Nigel Molesworth's
CYNICAL TENDENCY

Nigel Molesworth's
CYNICAL TENDENCY

Being a Satire of Sorts Set in the Quite Soon

Ian Strathcarron

Published by Affable Media Ltd
Hampshire

ISBN 978-1-911397-71-7

Cover design Felicity Price-Smith
Typeset by Vivian Head

FOREWORD
by Charlemagne Arbuthnot

When Nigel Molesworth's people contacted my people about writing this foreword, I was at first reluctant to say the least. I had met Molesworth at the odd, very odd, St Custard's reunion over the years and although he seemed a likeable enough fellow, I could never get over the fact that in his schoolboy writings he constantly referred to my father Sigismund Arbuthnot as the 'mad maths master'. Now there is no doubt that he was mad, quite mad, mad as a box of frogs as it happens, but in the eccentric rather than angry sense of the word. He was indeed the maths master, but the juxtaposition of the three words 'mad, maths and master' together gives an altogether false impression of a man who was not only fortunate enough to be named after a Holy Roman Emperor himself, but had the good sense to name his son and heir, my good self, after one too. The fact that he put out straw on the hot plates for his racing pigeons to sleep on is entirely irrelevant. Whether or not they actually flew any faster as a result could never be proved either way, something that worried him enormously.

Now Molesworth being a cynical fellow I expect asked me to write this foreword not because I'm a brilliant foreword writer, in fact this is my maiden voyage in this regard, but because he hoped my world famous fact-checking agency would be able to track down the mysterious author, Ian Strathcarron. Early results showed there was an Ian Strathcarron sitting in the House of Lords as Lord Strathcarron of Banchor, but he is a renowned dimwit and incapable of writing such a splendid satire. When interviewed he did, however, seem genuinely cross that someone would impost him and begged me to keep my team informed of our investigations.

However, next I had a stroke of luck. One of my neighbours' daughters is understudying at the Royal Shakespeare Company and at a barbeque in their garden I overheard her tell the story which brought me closer to finding out who is the impostor. The RSC were the on-board entertainment on *Queen Mary II* on one of her New York to Southampton voyages, and as part of the package they invite passengers to attend their workshops and rehearsals during the day as well as the performances in the evenings. She told how on the first day out, after their first workshop, this chap came up to the cast and, full of enthusiasm, told them how they had saved the day as he was stuck plotting a book and now he knew it had to be a play. She didn't think much more about it at the time, but over the next week this chap joined in every workshop and attended every rehearsal and performance and was such an enthusiastic participant that on the last night the cast invited him backstage to join in the final celebrations. They then discovered about the play he was writing, which was to be a political satire.

At the words 'political satire' I wandered over to ask her more about all of this. 'He was ever so nice,' she said, 'owned a publishing company and had already written a dozen books, the two most recent ones being a whole life biography of Bertie Wooster and a Victorian crime thriller written under the pseudonym Sherlock Holmes. This time he wanted a change from writing about fictional characters and so he had begun writing this docudrama about the famously successful St Custard's old boys, but it was at the time of Boris and Liz and you really couldn't make up what was going on as it was of course, as he said, beyond satire.'

'And what did he look like, this author?' I asked.

She then proceeded to describe somebody who looks remarkably similar to the aforementioned Ian Strathcarron, but as I and my world famous fact checking agency has already established that it couldn't be him, the author's identity has to remain a mystery.

But back to the book and the play, and back to my foreword. While Molesworth's view of my father is well known, less well known is that my father also kept a diary about his time at St Custard's. In this, in which he spells out his views of Molesworth, Fotherington-Thomas, Peason and Grabber and the rest of them too, Gillibrand and the vile headmaster Grimes who seldom paid my father and was motivated more by embezzlement than education. In fact, he despised the very concept of education, especially when it was wasted, as he saw it, on such revolting schoolboys as were in his care.

My father could be said to be one of those people who while highly intelligent have no brains at all, because he had the four heroes in the work down as complete wastrels who would never amount to anything, whereas as we now know they have all been phenomenally successful in the political realm.

The big question of course is how much of this satire is destined to become reality. With the benefit of foresight I can see Molesworth taking his famous Abstract Aims slightly more seriously than he's letting on in the book and the play. Beyond that, I can't divulge or will be straining into spoiler territory on the remote off-chance that anyone will be reading this foreword before they read the book or see the play. For me, I must confess I haven't read the book and have no intention of doing so, but I have attended the play's rehearsals and thought it was all mindless enough piffle that it might just appeal to the modern audience, cauterised as they are by political scandal, failure and lies. And so I wish it well, if only to confound my father, the 'mad maths master' Sigmund Artbuthnot, RIP.

CAST LIST
(4m/4f) in order of appearance

Grimes, St. Custard's headmaster [played by George Molesworth]

Timothy Peason, leader of the Labour Party

Basile (ex-Basil) Fotherington-Thomas, leader of the Green Party

Grabber, Prime Minister and leader of the Conservative Party

Nigel Molesworth, 'Molesworth 1' professional contrarian, founder of the Cynical Tendency, Twitter account and YouTube channel, new MP and future PM

George Molesworth, 'Molesworth 2' annoying younger brother, Nigel's number two

Infanta Roar-Ripping, outside broadcaster [played by Rowena Jones]

Jacob Jobsworth, town clerk for Rotten-under-Neath [played by King Charles]

Marjory MacDougal, leader of the Scottish Nationalist Party

Rowena Jones, leader of Plaid Cymru

Sheila O'Flattery, leader of Sinn Fein

King Charles III

PROLOGUE

Four schoolboys in school caps on chairs: Molesworth 1, Grabber, Peason and Fotherington-Thomas: NIGEL, GRABBER, PEASON and BASIL.

One headmaster standing, with mortar and gown and cane: Grimes, played by GEORGE.

GRIMES   Well, you horrible little boys, not you Grabber, the others, it's the end of 1964 and the end of your time here at St. Custard's. We've done our best with you, but I fear the worst, not for you Grabber, I'm talking about the others. In keeping with modern practice I have to offer you career advice, so help me God. Not that He will. Last week I had to tell you the facts of life, but all you did was snigger and giggle like a bunch of fairy schoolgirls, and we don't like fairy schoolgirls, do we? What don't we like?

ALL FOUR Fairy schoolgirls, sir.

GRIMES   That's right. That's how it should be. Now I'm going to tell you what to do with the rest of your lives, so you better listen or it will be one last swipe round the earhole. Got it?

ALL FOUR Yes, sir.

GRIMES   Right, you first Peason. Stand when I talk to you, boy.

(Peason stands)

You're the worst of all worlds, Peason, a horrible little swot and a stinking little turd? What are you?

PEASON   A horrible little swot and a stinking little turd, sir.

GRIMES   That's right. The only thing you're any good at is lying, and smirking like now, wipe that smile off your face when I'm talking to you, boy' And shirking. You've no chance of making anything of yourself, so I suggest you go into the clergy, where all you have to do is talk a load of nonsense in Latin and pass the hat around. Even you can't mess that up. Do your people know any vicars?

PEASON   No, sir.

GRIMES   Well, I do. Fotherington-Thomas's pater is an archbishop. Is that not right, Fotherington-Thomas?

BASIL   Yes, sir.

GRIMES   Yes, sir. Well you tell him that an old boy here needs a job and you sort it out. Old school tie, you'll all be getting one of those. And when you see another boy wearing it, you will help him out. No questions. That's what we do, look after each other and sod the rest of them. All together now.

ALL FOUR   Look after each other and sod the rest of them, sir.

GRIMES   That's right. That's how it should be. Any questions, Peason?

PEASON   Will I have to learn more Latin, sir, I was hoping to give it up?

GRIMES   That's a typical example of the shirking tendency I'm talking about. Sit down you fool, next Fotherington-Thomas.

(Peason sits, Fotherington-Thomas stands)

GRIMES   I won't be sad to see the back of you either, prancing around like a fairy all day, talking to the clouds and the sky. The sun and the moon too for all I know. You need to get a grip boy, join the Army, that'll make a man out of you. A bit of discipline, God knows I've tried to beat it into you. All you do is cry like a girl. What's all you do?

BASIL   Cry like a girl, sir.

GRIMES   That's right, cry like a girl and I've told you often enough the beatings will continue till you stop crying every time you get your whacks. A good regimental sergeant major will sort you out with a proper kick up the arse. My old regiment, the 44th Detestables are expecting you, and they know what to expect. Any questions, Fotherington-Thomas?

BASIL   Can I join the Navy, sir?

GRIMES   I see. A bit of rum, bum and concertina is it? I might have guessed the deviant tendency was behind all this. No, you can't. Sit down you great wet whoopsy, next Grabber.

(Fotherington-Thomas sits, Grabber stands)

GRIMES   Ah, Grabber, our beloved head boy. And I say this not just because your pater paid for the new Grabber Gymnasium and Swimming Pool and your mater consecrated the new Grabber Concert Hall and Assembly Room, welcome as both additions to the St. Custard's facilities are. You have only a bright future ahead of you, my boy, go into the family firm Grabber Inc. and conquer the world. Tell them you've been to St. Custard's, St. Custard's where your glorious career started. And when the next generation of Grabbers appear, I trust you'll put them down at birth.

NIGEL   Put them down at birth, sir, you mean strangle them?

GRIMES   You horrible little boy, you'd normally get three well-aimed juicy ones on the backside for that. What would you get?

NIGEL   Three well-aimed juicy ones on the backside, sir.

GRIMES   That's right, that's how it should be, but I'm in a good mood today, seeing the backside of you lot, not you Grabber, the others. Now then, any questions?

GRABBER   Yes sir, can I have my tuck box back, and filled up with tuck again?

GRIMES   Of course, of course, a splendid example of the greed-is-good tendency. And help yourself to any of the other boys' tuck that takes your fancy. They'll have me to answer to if they give you any backchat. Sit down, boy. Next, Molesworth 1.

(Grabber sits, Molesworth 1 stands)

              We've had some horrible little beasts through St. Custard's, but you are without doubt the most horrible and beastly of them all. What are you?

NIGEL   Horrible and beastly, sir. The most horrible and beastly of them all.

GRIMES   That's right. The most horrible and beastly of them all. Not only do you refuse to do any swotting yourself, you stop any other boy who wants to swot from swotting too. As for games, you prefer to hide in the bushes rather than get your legs broken like a proper boy. No, my only regret is that your parents have decided to take the even more revolting, if that were possible, Molesworth 2 away from here too, just after I'd booked my holiday to Benidorm. Do you know what you want to do with yourself in later life?

NIGEL   No, sir.

GRIMES   No, sir. You are useless and unemployable, deceitful and dishonest. You're also a doubter, a good-for-nothing and a cynic, a perfect example of that most regrettable of all tendencies, the cynical tendency. There is only one option open to you, go into politics, become a politician. Any questions?

NIGEL   Yes sir, can I smash up Fotherington-Thomas one last time before I go home to mater and pater?

GRIMES   Very well, if you must, Grabber and Peason, you can join in too. I'll watch. Just for old times' sake. But make it quick, it's nearly opening time.

ACT ONE

Scene 1

In Rotten-under-Neath village hall the constituency result in the general election is about to be announced. It is early hours of the morning.

Centre stage is a female TV reporter INFANTA [played by ROWENA] talking to the audience as if to camera. Back of stage unlit is JOBSWORTH [played by Peason].

INFANTA

(Breathless with excitement, headphones and mic)

Thank you Andrew, and yes here at Rotten-under-Neath there's tremendous excitement as any moment now we are expecting the result of this 2026 general election. The answer everyone wants to know is: Where is the star attraction, the candidate Nigel Molesworth? Wherever he is, he is not here, I can tell you that. Has Nigel, founder of the Cynical Tendency, succeeded at his first attempt to win a constituency seat? Has the scourge of the political class become an MP and what trouble awaits them now, that's what we are all so keen to find out. Any moment now the clerk here MR JOSEPH JOBSWORTH is getting ready to announce the results. I am told he's going to announce the results whether Nigel Molesworth is here or not. I can't wait and everyone here is really excited, but wait is what we'll have to do, so in the meantime Andrew it's back to you. No hang on I can see Mr Jobsworth getting ready now! Oh no, and here is Nigel Molesworth himself. Will Jobsworth wait for him? We just don't know, it's too exciting. Let me see if I can catch a word with Nigel.

(Nigel enters, flashbulbs flashing)

INFANTA Nigel, Nigel, over here. Infanta Roar-Ripping from UKTV. Everyone's been asking, where have you been?

NIGEL I had trouble finding it, I've never been to Rotten before and the traffic was terrible.

INFANTA Do you think you're going to win?

NIGEL I don't know, and I'm not terribly bothered. If I win, I win, if not, not. Now if you'll excuse me, I think I better go and ...

INFANTA But you must be excited Nigel, your own party Cynical Tendency has candidates all over the country. Aren't you worried about how they are doing?

NIGEL I'm not worried about anything. I'm sure my candidates all feel the same. They're all stand-up comedians, that's how they got the gig. Like me, I'm sure they are happy enough going back to obscurity once this is all over.

INFANTA   That's some obscurity. The sell-out tours, the most subscribed to political channel on YouTube.

NIGEL   It's not really a political channel, just 17 million people amazed and bemused by all the hubris we are living through? Now I suppose I better go on stage to hear the result.

INFANTA   Looks like they've started already without you, Nigel.

Scene 2
Same set, results clerk JACOB JOBSWORTH [Played by Peason] now centre stage lit, Infanta unlit.

JOBSWORTH

(Flat and wooden)

I, Joseph Jobsworth of the borough of Rotten-under-Neath, being the duly certified returning officer for said borough, do hereby solemnly declare the results of this constituency election:

Simon Sickbag, Conservative Party 1,350 votes

(Tiny cheer off)

Brenda Clotshot, Labour Party 1,360 votes

(Small cheer off)

Sally McSilly, Mad Hatter Delinquents Party, 4,375 votes

(Medium cheer off)

Nigel Molesworth, Cynical Tendency 11,567 votes.

(Big cheer off)

Quiet please. I do hearby declare that Nigel Molesworth is the constituency MP for Rotten-under-neath.

INFANTA

(Close to meltdown)

Well, there we have it, the most sensational result you can imagine, absolutely sensational and ground-breaking and will the world ever be the same again, that's what everyone here wants to know. As you can see behind me, Nigel's supporters are cheering and clapping and any moment now I'm sure he will make his acceptance speech.

NIGEL   Friends, voters, clerks, helpers, media, thank you. As many of you will know, this is the first time I've actually been in this constituency and it's also quite likely to be the last. I will, however, represent you in parliament to see how they look after themselves first and foremost and report back on it on my YouTube channel and live shows.

INFANTA   Have you a message for us, Nigel?

NIGEL   Resist! And if you really want to know what's going on, follow the money, it is only ever about the money. Who is paying those who want to control you and why are they paying them? Answer, to monetise you in ways you don't know and in ways you won't know are even happening to you. Don't trust any of them, ever, especially if they are in government, global institutions, multinationals, the media or quangos, they only have one thing on their minds: to increase their power by reducing yours. Trust only yourself. For the rest, resist!

INFANTA   And where are you going now?

NIGEL   Back to London, if I can ever find my way out of here. Where are we again?

INFANTA   Rotten-under-Neath. Even I know that Nigel. Well, Andrew, there you have it, an absolute sensation, never have we seen anything like it before, 17 million Cynical Tendency YouTube subscribers voting in constituencies across the UK. No mention of the Tendency's famous Abstract Aims tonight, no need to really, everyone knows them by now and they have obviously struck a chord with the public who have voted for the Cynics in their droves quite frankly, and all the other minority parties. And I'm just hearing with most results in by now, we have got the latest exit poll.

(Projected onto a screen)

> Conservative Party 220
> Labour Party 150
> Cynical Tendency 146
> Scottish Nationalist Party 55
> Green Party 21
> Plaid Cymru 9
> Sinn Fein 9
> Ulster Forever Party 6
> Cornish Independence Now 3
> Liberal Democrat (provisional Stalinist)
>   Party 3
> Yorkshire Independence Soon 2
> Ethnic British Diaspora Party 1
> M25 Anticlockwise Priority Coalition 1

INFANTA

(Very slowly giving time for audience to read)

> That's too complicated to work out right now, all the different permutations, it could go any which way but it looks to me like the new MP for Rotten-Under-Neath Nigel Molesworth might well hold the balance of power. I can't believe it's happening. We are in for a rocky ride ahead, Andrew, this is one of the most sensational nights I can ever remember. This is Infanta Roar-Ripping, UKTV, in Rotten-under-Neath handing you back to the studio.

Scene 3
The next morning, same set.

Sheila, Rowena and Marjory spot lit on Zooms to each other, with Irish, Welsh and Scottish posters or flags behind them, talking directly from behind desks to the audience as if to laptop screen camera.

MARJORY

(In centre as the ringleader)

> Well that worked out pretty well for all of us, wouldn't you say girls? A real triumph of a night. We've got the English on the run now, just where we want the cheating bastards.

SHEILA Amazing, Marjory, I really think we are on our way, a united Ireland at last. A dream come true. What made the difference was the prods, hundreds of thousands of orange prods voted with us proper paddies. They'd rather be part of the cesspit that is Eire than the cesspit that is Britain. Don't quote me on that girls, about Eire.

MARJORY Ah, excuse me there Sheila, England is the cesspit, don't bring us into it. There are no cesspits in Scotland. We have not only banned them, anyone who even thinks about a cesspit in their home is in trouble. And that applies to motorhomes too.

ROWENA I gave my acceptance speech in Welsh, the English media acted like I was speaking a foreign language. Well, at this rate they'll all have to learn it soon enough. Look, I don't want to cause trouble or anything, Marjory, but you're a bit stuck up there in haggis land on 55 seats are you not, same as last time if I'm not mistaken?

MARJORY It's the Highlands. Still full of English and their lackeys. They don't hate the English like good Scots should. And now this new Cynical Tendency have three seats, all in Glasgow, our patch. I mean, who the hell are they?

ROWENA Same in Cardiff, right on our patch too.

MARJORY They are a cancer, we need to cut them out before everyone's voting for them. So what shall we three do, we should definitely form an alliance? An Independence Alliance. Push for three referenda, we three all push, push, push.

ROWENA I reckon we've got 73 seats between us. If we get together with Labour and the Cornish and Yorkshires and the M25 nutter and the Ethnos we can easily form a government.

SHEILA And the Greens. Although they'd rather freeze to death than light a fire. Could we not get them on board? But getting together with Labour, I don't know. That Peason is a weasel. A slimy one too. I met him in Belfast once, wouldn't even buy himself a drink, let alone the rest of us. I mean, what's the point of a politico who can't stand a round?

MARJORY Peason? He is a weasel for sure Sheila, no problem with that, but he'd never agree, it would be the end of Labour, although they hate being British, and hate the English as much as we do. We've already knocked them sideways in Scotland, they've only got the English inner cities and the rest of the English would never forgive them. No, that one won't fly, unfortunately.

ROWENA Same with us really. Labour's on the run, the more they hate the English the more the

Welsh vote for us. What about the Tories, scum that they are. Means must, and all that.

MARJORY The Tories, over my dead body is my gut instinct. But, as you say if needs must. I know Grabber. He's a fat piece of nasty but honestly dishonest. He'd sell his grandma for a pound of oaties. The Highland English up here would go mad, which would be fun. But they didn't used to be called the Conservative and Unionist Party for nothing, no, Rowena they'll never be seen to break up the Union. What else have we got?

SHEILA Well I've never shagged a Tory, not knowingly, so don't ask me. So that just leaves us with Cynical Tendency. I don't know anything about them at all. These Abstract Aims, what are they when they're at home. It's all done on the social and telly as far as I can tell. Does anyone know this Nigel Molesworth?

ROWENA No.

MARJORY No.

SHEILA No from me neither. Do we even know how to contact him?

ROWENA No.

MARJORY No.

SHEILA No, me neither, maybe Twitter, he's got a zillion followers. It's not even as though he's got a political party, he calls it a movement. And not a bowel movement. Sorry to mention that.

ROWENA Even if we do contact him, do we know if he will play ball, maybe he's a Unionist like the others?

MARJORY I'm sure he is, why wouldn't he be? Cynics, that's a joke. If he wants a lesson in cynicism he should come up here, see how we've been subsidising the English for years.

SHEILA We could all say that, Marjory, centuries in our case, stealing all the land so they say, breeding horses like there's no tomorrow, shooting everything and everyone that moves left, right and centre.

MARJORY Shooting. Yes. Yes, you've just reminded me. Now I think about it, I met someone recently who went shooting with Molesworth's younger brother George. It was one of our backers, the Earl of Glencormack.

ROWENA You've got an English toff backing you?

MARJORY	Scottish toff, as it happens. File under useful idiot.
SHEILA	Now that sounds promising. I never meet any of our backers, they're all abroad, mostly in the US.
ROWENA	You're lucky, none of our backers are that rich. A fiver here and a tenner around the pubs is all we can do. We make more on a bingo round. What are they shooting anyway?
MARJORY	Birds I suppose, I've never actually been up there.
ROWENA	So you know how to contact him? This George Molesworth.
MARJORY	Through our tame Earl. Then I'm just a couple of phone calls away. But what's in it for Molesworth? We could offer him Home Secretary.
SHEILA	How about Foreign Secretary?
MARJORY	Does he even like foreigners?
ROWENA	Or Chancellor of the Exchequer. Can he even add up?
MARJORY	Can any of them? The Scots invented mathematics.
SHEILA	I thought that was the Arabs.

MARJORY   It was, the Scots of the desert, they just call themselves Arabs to annoy us.

Scene 4

Nigel's flat backdrop, without two of the desks. GEORGE is scratching his arse, NIGEL is working at the desk. PEASON enters soon.

(Entry phone rings, George answers it.)

GEORGE   It's Tim Peason, Bro. Never guess what he wants.

NIGEL   What's taken him so long?

(Peason enters)

PEASON   Molesworth 1, Molesworth 2 and Peason, the three great friends from St Custard's Form 3B, who would have thought it?

GEORGE   I wasn't your great friend, I thought you were a swot. And I wasn't in Form 3B.

PEASON   Well, that's all in the past. Bygones be bygones, that's what I always say. Nigel, you've done so well in the election. Congratulations.

NIGEL   And to you too, Tim, coming second in a general election is what you've devoted the whole of your adult life to. The Labour Party is lucky to have you leading it, even if you are the most Tory person I've ever met.

PEASON   It's a responsibility, something you've devoted your whole life to avoiding.

NIGEL   True. Responsibility is an overrated trait best left to others. You remember last summer in Paxos with all the families and I said I was thinking of turning Cynical Tendency into a movement and putting up candidates, just for the fun of it?

PEASON   I do, only too well.

NIGEL   Sarah and Cassandra shuddered at the thought that you and I might one day be having this conversation about forming a government.

PEASON   Sarah is at home pretending it's not happening and Cassie I presume is as far away from the election as she possibly can be?

NIGEL   Salmon fishing in Norway. Not even a phone signal. So let me guess, you want to form an alliance, or coalition I suppose?

PEASON   It's the only route to power. I can't team up with the Nationalists, break up the Union, my Bollinger Bolshies would kill me. I can't team up with Grabber and the Tories, my Trots would kill me. You're my only hope. Luckily you're also my oldest friend.

NIGEL   Team up with me and the Cynical Tendency? Your public sector would kill you too. It's all you've got left. They'd never wear it, not after what I've been saying about the overpaid, underworked ...

PEASON   But does it really matter what our voters think? I mean, really? They'll just have to put up with it. It's only for a few years. It's their fault after all, not voting decisively enough for any of us.

NIGEL   So, you and I, we're their least worst option?

PEASON   Well, yes, if you put it like that. We've got five years to prove them wrong, five years in which we could both do rather nicely for ourselves. And I don't believe your voters aren't interested in power, otherwise why would they have bothered to vote?

NIGEL   They bothered to vote to stop people like you ruling over them. I would too if I was one of my voters. And I didn't even vote, it only encourages you lot.

PEASON   But they've got to have someone rule over them, the broad masses. Why not you and me?

NIGEL   So let me get this straight, if the Cynics team up with Labour, and you're offering me Prime Minister, what would you be?

PEASON   Prime Minister? Who said anything about you being Prime Minister?

NIGEL   I did. Just now.

PEASON   But Nigel, be reasonable. I got more MPs than you, only just, but still. I called you, you didn't call me. That must count for something. I didn't devote my whole life to the Labour Party, to this great movement of ours, to play second fiddle to someone who is basically an anarchist.

NIGEL   So you would rather have no power at all, than be number two to someone else?

PEASON   It's not someone else Nigel, it's you. My oldest friend. We could never be friends again.

NIGEL   Maybe, maybe not, but unlike me you've obviously given this some thought. So what's the trade? You want to be Prime Minister. Don't I have some sort of public duty to prevent it? I love you and Sarah dearly, but you couldn't even run a bath.

PEASON   So what? Neither can any of the others.

NIGEL   Grabber can. Even I have to admit it's not his fault we're in the mess we're in.

PEASON   All Grabber can do is line his pockets. And if I only achieve one thing in office, it's to nobble Grabber. He's the most frightful shit, go on, admit it.

NIGEL   True, but even that does show some level of competence.

PEASON   What you're really asking is what's in it for you.

NIGEL   I'm not. But what is? In it for me.

PEASON   I know you Nigel, and I've thought it all through. I've got the perfect job for you. Foreign Secretary, even Foreign and Commonwealth Secretary. You've always liked foreigners. And I don't think even you have got anything against the Commonwealth. You could swan around the world in an Air Force jet, get plastered at exotic jamborees at other peoples' expense, pontificate till you're blue in the face. You know you love an audience, Nigel. Your favourite place has always been a pub with an audience. Then God invented YouTube. You won't actually have to do any work, I can guarantee you that. Snidebottom can do the actual work, you'll just be lending me your MPs. From what I've seen, they're a bunch of misfit stand-ups anyway and I don't suppose they care as long as they get paid.

NIGEL   True, but there's a flaw in your plan, Tim. I don't want to be Foreign Secretary. Even Foreign and Commonwealth Secretary. I don't want anything to do with any of it.

GEORGE   Go on, Bro, take it. Sounds like a laugh. I can be your deputy dog, air miles city. Foreign leg over, what's not to like?

PEASON   You should listen to Molesworth 2, Molesworth 1.

NIGEL   So should you, you might have some idea what you're getting yourself into if I follow his advice.

PEASON   So it's a no? A no for now anyway.

NIGEL   Yes, Tim, it's a no, as in *never* no. And I don't mean you never know.

PEASON   One thing I do know is you'll change your mind. I know you Nigel, I've known you ever since you were Molesworth 1, the curse of St. Custard's, the scourge of Form 3B. Anyway, now I must go or I'll be late for the shadow cabinet. *À bientôt* as we used to say in Latin Lit.

(Peason leaves)

GEORGE   Same old Peason, always on the scrounge. He's right though, you'd be mad to turn this down, what a blag.

(Entry phone rings, George answers it)

Scene 5
Nigel's flat. NIGEL, GEORGE and BASILE.

(Entry phone rings, George answers it)

GEORGE   Come on up.

(One hand over the mouthpiece)

You'll never believe it, it's that old Green poofter Fotherington-Thomas.

NIGEL   George, I keep telling you, he's no longer an old Green gay, she's now a new Green woman, he's made the switcheroo. Our old friend Basil is now our new friend Basile. Is she on her way up?

GEORGE   Yup, here comes the bride.

(Basile enters overhearing)

(Ignoring George)

35

BASILE   He's such a tease. A political bride I suppose he means? I thought I'd pop round, I'm only round the corner, then I saw that horrible swot Peason on his way out. I can only guess what he wants, I don't think so Nigel. Not your scene at all. Anyway, we both did a lot better than expected, didn't we? Who would've thought it, the curse of St. Custard's and the weed of St. Custard's, on top of the world, what joy! But now to matters of a greenish hue. Oh Nigel, dear Nigel, you have no idea how soon the world will end unless we mend our ways. No more clouds, no more sky. We need to take the first tiny step to saving it and ourselves. If you would be President I would be Vice-President of the Ecology. But you must give me a free hand. These dreams of the world on fire are really most disturbing. Don't worry Nigel, dear Nigel, I have thought it all through. I have 21 MPs and you have 146. My MPs are all quite mad, and I wouldn't give a job to any of them and I certainly wouldn't expect you to. Yours are all stand-up comedians, I hear that was your only requirement of them and of course signing up to your wonderful Abstract Aims. No, I'll just be Vice-President of the Environmental Ecology and then I can start being really useful saving the planet. Can we roll in all the independence people? By my calculation if we have their 30 MPs we will have 198. I don't care about independence, and I'm sure

36

you don't Nigel, you've never really bothered about anything petty like that. Big picture Nigel that's what you are. I'm more interested in the whole planet really rather than borders and countries, yuk, it's all so childish. I mean the M25 whatever they're called, what a funny idea that is, as though they could build a kind of fresh air bubble around the M25 of all things. Anyway, we got three green MPs in London and they've only got one, so ya boo sucks to them. Oh and the Liberal Stalinists, they'll come on board our magic bus. It could all be so wonderful Nigel, dear Nigel, what do you think?

NIGEL   Basile, my dear woman, I've known you long enough to say I think you're stark staring bonkers. Just like the rest of your gang. So in one sense that's a promising start to this coalition you have in mind, because as you say, my lot are too. But you seem to think that I want to be Prime Minister as much as you want to be Environment Minister or whatever you call it, but you're wrong. I have absolutely no interest in sorting out this mess at all. I'm a bit like you Greens, spouting off nonsense from the sidelines safe in the knowledge I'm never going to have to do anything about it.

BASILE   Oh dear, so why did you go through all the bother of making a party and put up all those stand-up candidates? It was bad enough for me, but at least the party already existed and after I gave them all that money, well they could hardly refuse having me at the helm. And they are such lovely people by and large, although they do have their disagreements. Sometimes it can get quite heated up, I can tell you. There's a new moderate wing causing quite a stir. All this new talk, things may not be quite as bad as we have been saying, science this and science that. I mean Nigel, where would we be if things aren't quite as bad as we've been saying? If the world isn't going to end soon, what's the point? Where is the good in that?

NIGEL   It's hard for me to know where to start. But do go on, you're writing my next script.

BASILE   How are you off for money, Nigel? I don't mean you you, the Nigel you, I mean the party you. You won't be nearly as rich as me, even if you did have to work for it. All that advertising money and all those full stadiums. You're rich, but what about the Cynics? Every party could do with some more money. Since I used my own money to take over the Greens, new money has simply poured in from global institutions worried about the planet. There's this new one from Oslo, the Global Settlement Foundation, they say they'll give me anything I want, just keep spreading the word, I do it so well they tell me. I could ask them for some money and give it to you. They are very respectable, you've nothing to worry about in that departmernt, they go to that Davos party every year. They've invited me to go next year.

NIGEL   By private jet like a good Emma Thompson I hope. I went there by private jet last year to make a YouTube, and you could practically start a private air force with the number of PJs there. I used to think PJs meant pyjamas.

BASILE   Oh, they haven't mentioned that. They'll have to get me there somehow.

GEORGE   I'll go, I've always wanted to go to in a private jet, me.

BASILE   Oh George, you're such a tease, it wouldn't take off with you in it. So come on Nigel, dear Nigel, President Nigel, what do you say?

NIGEL   I say no. Or as you would say, a big fat no with none of the trimmings, as in no, not now, not ever. Now, if you'll excuse me, I have to write my next script.

BASILE

(Flouncing off)

Until you change your mind. I'm off too, fish to fry. You're impossible, both of you.

GEORGE   He still makes me sick.

NIGEL   She still makes you sick. How come?

GEORGE   Just gives me the creeps, you must admit he's a bit weird.

NIGEL   None the worse for that, I think she's less annoying now than he was then.

(Entry phone rings)

GEORGE   Christ' Who now? It's like Piccadilly Circus in here.

NIGEL   I know who. Begins with a G.

(George answers it)

❧

Scene 6
Same set. NIGEL, GEORGE and GRABBER.

GEORGE   Come on up.

(One hand over the mouthpiece)

You're right, he does. Begin with a G. Grabber, no less.

GRABBER   Molesworths I and II, hells bells I haven't seen you two chizzes since St Custard's. You know I bought it, it's now a juvenile delinquent centre. Always was, of course, but now it's all mine and you know who pays the fees? The government. And you know who runs the government? I'll tell you, it's me.

NIGEL   So what are you going to do with it?

GRABBER   St. Custard's? Put in some tough management. The existing headmaster is a wuss, welfare this and welfare that. Load of bollocks in my not so humble opinion. Know any good thugs for the job? Steer them my way if so. Who was that going out? I recognise her from somewhere.

GEORGE   That was *Miss* Fotherington-Thomas, used to be *Master* Fotherington-Thomas, was a poofter, now a lezzo.

GRABBER   I thought it was the Green woman from the telly, scrubs up better live than on the box. Almost beddable. Almost. I wouldn't give her one. We'll be seeing her in the House soon, unfortunately, along with all the other new rabble of misfits. I hear she's rich from an inheritance. Her uncle. No children, just a niece or nephew or whatever she was or is. A big one. Oil, from the old days. Did she try to buy you off?

NIGEL   Yes, Grabber she did. Money and office. Are you going to try to buy me off?

GEORGE   Go on, Grabber, make us an offer.

GRABBER   No need, losers, I've already bought you. Lock, stock and smoking gun. Or at least I've bought your management company. World Talent Management is now part of Grabber Inc. As of three days ago when I saw the in-house polling and knew how well you were doing. Deal just gone through. They should never have taken the company public, great mistake, rule number one. I'm private me, as private as a skunk's arse. Of course as PM it's got nothing to do with me. But my offshore holding now owns your onshore holding. Rule number two, never do anything onshore, I'm so far offshore I'm over the horizon. I'm Tony Blair with brass knobs on, me.

NIGEL   Grabber, the problem for you is I really don't care. Unless you buy YouTube, Twitter and every large arena in the land, and even you can't do that. I've got a dozen management companies lining up to represent me if you kick me off of World Talent Management. So what's the point? What's the point of anything you do?

GRABBER   The point is Molesworth 1, we all have our price. In spite of what you say, it would be more than troublesome for you to be kicked out of World Talent, especially if they were indiscreet enough to spread rumours about why they kicked you out. Drugs and orgies, I hear. Underage females of the opposite sex, no doubt. Doesn't matter if it's true or not. Tabloid fodder, and I own one of them too.

NIGEL   A race to the bottom.

GRABBER   Exactly so. Well done, you're learning, On the other hand, if we can do a deal on the political stuff, as a favour to an old friend I can halve World Talent's commission rate so you would be even richer than you are already. Not as rich as me, but still. And I wouldn't have to create any scandal. Be sensible Molesworth. I'll cut you two deals in one, professional and political.

NIGEL   But I'm not interested in either. I really don't care.

GRABBER   Of course you care, man, or you wouldn't have bothered with it all. Everyone wants power, it's human nature. Power is money, that's human nature too, monetising power. Home Secretary for you, I can see you now. Massive great department and I'll increase the budget by 25%. You don't have to do much, I'll put in one of my people, Ponsonby-Smythe. He's halfway sensible, he'll do the work. Doing the work means dealing with the civil service. I wouldn't expect you to do that, not after what you've been saying about the lazy gits.

NIGEL And if I don't?

GRABBER Then my dear old mucker, I will screw you. I will screw you slowly, every which way you never even imagined. Your life will be more than uncomfortable, it simply won't be worth living. This isn't a choice between easy street where you live now and doing without the croissant with your latte, it's a choice between professional ruin and political triumph. I haven't seen you since St Custard's, but you were an annoying little scrote then, and you're starting to annoy me again now.

NIGEL And you can huff and puff and bullshit and bluster all you like, Grabber. I'm invincible, because I'm not playing the game. I can survive without you, but the way the votes worked out you can't survive without me. So let's have a little renegotiation.

GRABBER Meaning?

NIGEL I don't want to be Home Secretary. I don't want to be Chancellor of the Exchequer. I don't want to be Foreign Secretary, or any other puffed up nonentity you want me to be. But the Cynical Tendency's Abstract Aims, that started off as a bit of a whimsy, soon turned into something serious about how to clear up the mess we're in now. A mess that you, and people like you, created. If you adopt my Abstract Aims as your policies, you can have my votes. If you renege, I renege. And then if the laws of mathematics haven't changed much since Sigismund Arbuthnot's day, you're stuffed.

GRABBER I don't even know what these Abstract Aims are. Will I be richer or poorer? Pretty basic question, which is it?

NIGEL Everyone will be richer, including you.

GRABBER I'm not interested in everyone. And anyway, these Abstract Aims, if they're so great, why didn't I think of them? What are they, anyway?

NIGEL Look on my website. You have until 9 o'clock tomorrow morning to agree. Or it's Peason as PM.

GRABBER OK, I'll have my people look at it. At them. But bear this in mind. I'm the only game in town. Peason's a loser, Fotherington-Thomas is a wuss. The Nats want to break up the Union. Surely even you care about the Union?

NIGEL   I couldn't care less about the Union. The Scots hate us, they cost us a fortune, they're always moaning and whinging about something or other. The Welsh are just as bad, although they're slightly less annoying, only because there are fewer of them. And the Irish have always hated us, no idea why and the northern lot cost us a fortune too. All four countries would be happier and England would be a lot richer, and we wouldn't have to put up with any of them.

GRABBER   You're right, but I've got to go through the motions of looking like I care. The whinging Scots are the worst. What a bunch of bastards. Anyway, let's say these Abstract Aims aren't so wonderful,who else have you got to turn to?

NIGEL   Nobody, I go back to the videos and the stadiums. You'll have to cobble up a deal with Peason.

GRABBER   Peason? That shining shitbag?

GEORGE   Nine o'clock Grabber. You better hurry, time is running out. Now piss off.

GRABBER   I won't forget this. Whatever happens, Molesworth 1, Molesworth 2 is toast. No one talks to me like that. And it's no deal all round. You can stick your Abstract Aims where they belong, up your arse.

(Grabber storms off)

GEORGE   Good riddance, he was always a thug.

NIGEL   Thug, yes.

(Rushing after Grabber)

Grabber, wait a minute, I have an idea for you.

⋘·⋅◉⋅·⋙

Scene 7
Same set. NIGEL and GEORGE.

GEORGE   Well bro, looks like we're in the pound seats here. We could really clean up, come on, even you can see it.

NIGEL   We could be in the pound seats, but we could also have a lot more fun pulling strings from the sidelines. Without being seen to be pulling strings from the sidelines. It will be educational. I don't suppose you have read Machiavelli?

GEORGE   Never heard of him. Mackey who?

NIGEL   The Prince would wait for increased chaos. Hold back awhile. Cause this increased chaos. The ferrets are in the sack. They will do what ferrets will do.

GEORGE   I've no idea what you're talking about.

NIGEL   Neither would the others. Desperadoes waiting for a train, every one of them. Anyway George, let's hear it, what would you do?

GEORGE   Grabber. Has to be Grabber. He's already Prime Minister. Peason's a soft sod and Fotherington-Thomas is a nancy-boy. Got to be Grabber. You won't even have to do any work. And he's as rich as that Greek chap Grimes was always banging on about.

NIGEL   Croesus?

GEORGE   No, the opera singer, Onassis. Or the other one. Who cares? He's your cheque book, name your price. You could sell the whole of Cynical Tendency, take a job as minister of something with government contracts and clean up big time. You've always said how they waste so much money, how they're all bent, now it's our turn to cash in. They can spend it our way, big time.

NIGEL   Yes George, but ...

GEORGE   What?

NIGEL   Grabber is as repellent now as he was in

form 3B at St. Custard's. Can you imagine having to deal with him every day? It's not just the boasting and the bullying and the bullshit. Actually it *is* just the boasting and the bullying and the bullshit. That's all there is to him.

GEORGE   OK, so if you don't like him, how about Tim? You often say Peason is your oldest friend in the world. At least you like him. And we could still clean up, I know you.

NIGEL   He is my oldest friend in the world and one of the reasons we never talk about politics, even though that is all he has ever done.

GEORGE   So?

NIGEL   So, that's hardly the ideal starting point for a coalition which is all about politics. In fact every day and night is going to be nothing but politics, politics, politics. Our friendship wouldn't survive the first day. Apart from that it annoys me that he's God's own Tory and only joined Labour as it was the easy option to the top.

GEORGE   So?

NIGEL   So, I dislike both parties equally. Anyway, the problem isn't really Tim, it's his lunatic MPs and activists. They can't agree about anything and hate each other more than they hate the British. He spends half his time trying to talk them out of committing political suicide. I could really do without it. As he would say, where's the upside. And I don't want to end up talking like him either.

GEORGE   Alright, but I think you're being a bit fussy. So what about Basil or Basile or whatever the fuck he calls himself these days?

NIGEL   George, sometimes...

GEORGE   You're right, maybe not.

NIGEL   And don't forget this was all an accident, a joke that went right. I never went into it to clean up as you put it, I'm cleaning up anyway. YouTube want me to start a new channel and my shows sell out at £75 a pop. And I don't have a care in the world. I'd quite like to keep it that way.

GEORGE   Including me?

NIGEL   Including you what?

GEORGE   Not a care in the world. Like you just said.

NIGEL   No, not including you, George. Of course I care about you, I care about Cassandra and Bertie and Rosie and the grandchildren. I'm not talking about people. I'm talking about life. Things.

GEORGE   But this is my big chance. You going into politics. I can do stuff behind the scenes for you that you can't do yourself. What else have I got? Flogging cars off Reg's forecourt? Sometimes helping you on location?

NIGEL   You're my road manager.

GEORGE   I'm your gofer. And don't forget you owe me. For what I did for Mum when you bogged off.

NIGEL   I haven't forgotten I owe you and I'll always be grateful for what you did. I've done my best over the years and I'm working on something for you now. But what you're asking is more than paying back a debt, it's a whole new life.

(Long silence)

Maybe there's a Plan D. We haven't met any of the Nationalists yet. At least we'll agree politically, which is more than can be said for any of the others. I think between us and the M25 guy and the mad Yorkies and the Cornish loonies, plus the LibDem Stalinists we could just about form a government.

GEORGE   Now you're talking sense.

NIGEL   Do we know any of them?

GEORGE   I went shooting with the Earl who funds the Scottish lot.

NIGEL   Good. Phone him, and get to speak to whatever her name is. Marjory. The one who reminds every man of his first wife. She'll know how to get hold of the others. Invite them round to the flat for drinks pronto.

GEORGE   Will do, then I'm off to the pub, it's been a busy morning. Want anything?

(Both leave stage in opposite directions)

Scene 8
NIGEL and GEORGE. CHARLES on stage, not yet spotlit, talking directly to the audience as if a camera.
(Laptop video rings)

(George enters, picking his noise, looking at the snot and eating it)

GEORGE   Bloody hell, who's that?

(Answers it)

              Molesworth.

CHARLES   Nigel, I'm sure you remember me. It's...

GEORGE   It's not Nigel, it's George. Who are you?

CHARLES   I'm Charles, don't you recognise my voice? Can you turn the video on? All will be revealed. Nigel and I ... just put him on.

GEORGE   No, fuck off. Charles who? He's busy anyway. There is an election on, in case you hadn't noticed.

CHARLES   That's why I'm calling. Now get me Nigel. Whoever you are. Now, please.

GEORGE

(Hands over phone)
                Fuck's sake.

(Shouting to off stage)

                Bro'! Bro'!

NIGEL

(Entering right)

                Yup.

GEORGE   Geezer called Charles on the phone. Says it's urgent.

NIGEL   Hello. Nigel Molesworth here.

CHARLES   Nigel, it's me, Charles.

NIGEL   One second please, just muting you.

(To George)

It's King Charles you moron, I'll put him on video, you stay off camera.

(Lights now on Charles)

(To the camera/audience)

Sorry about that, unintelligent staff syndrome. Hello again. We met last month at the BAFTAs.

CHARLES   We did. I gave you a prize. Can't remember which one. Best video was it?

NIGEL   Best subscriber channel.

CHARLES   That's the fellow. And I remembered you were at St Custard's while I was at Cheam. We played against each other at footie. I think we won, sorry about that.

NIGEL   I'm sure you did, St Custard's never won at anything. So, um, how can ... ?

CHARLES   Yes. it's about this election thingie. I think you hold what I'm told is called the balance of power, and I really hope you are going to do the decent thing. National interest, time for all good men, rally round the flag, if you get my drift.

NIGEL Not really my forte, decent thing, national interest, all good men, rally and the flag. I could give them a go, I suppose. What in particular have you in mind?

CHARLES The United Kingdom. United and Kingdom being the most important words.

NIGEL So not the 'the'?

CHARLES Eh? Ah, I see what you mean, no, not the 'the' just United and Kingdom. Don't worry about all that sort of thing, this is far more important. The point is, if you form a government, you must at all costs avoid collusion with the Nationalists, Scottish, Welsh or Irish, or any combination thereof.

NIGEL If I form a government. It's unlikely. It's undesirable. I wouldn't wish it on anybody. I'm totally unsuitable, so unsuitable I'm a-suitable. Governments are the cause of all problems.

CHARLES But you sound like an anarchist, man. There must be some form of government, otherwise how would we exist? Who would consult me? Whom would I advise?

NIGEL   The moment two people are stranded on a desert island some form of government evolves. That is human nature. Any fool knows that. I'm talking about the type of government we have now, centralised, the self-aggrandisement, the greed and the lust to control people's lives.

CHARLES   Very well. You may be right. I don't know about these things like you do, with your best subscriber channel and everything. Heavens, I gave you a prize for it, you must know more than me. But someone is going to have to form a government, and it's either going to be Grabber, Peason, Fotherington-Thomas or you. All old Saint Custardians as you will no doubt have gathered. According to you, the other three are all professional politicians, and between them they've got us into this mess in the first place. So I would rather it was you who gets us out of it. I'm hoping we might be able to come to some sort of arrangement.

NIGEL   Arrangement?

CHARLES   Arrangement, yes. Apart from forming a government and preserving the Union, there's also this damn petition.

NIGEL   Petition?

CHARLES   You must've heard about it man, it's already

got 300,000 signatures and has become some kind of national pastime. Thousands signing up every day. They don't know what they are doing, they're being duped.

NIGEL   To replace you with the Waleses. Yes, I have heard of it. Look, it's just the current thing, this month's bread and circus whipped up by the media. Forget it, that's what I always do. In a couple of weeks they'll think of new ways to wind up the mob. Probably have a pop at me again, but it only ever does me good.

CHARLES It's easy for you to say that, but this is what I do. I can't be replaced. Not just like that. I have to die first, that's the way things are. Always has been. This is where I hope we might come to the arrangement I have in mind. If you can form a government with one of your old school mates, I'll make you a knight, Sir Nigel Molesworth no less. Cassandra, I believe her name is, will be Lady M, I bet she'll love that, all the girls do, and when this whole ghastly fiasco is over I'll make sure you get a peerage, Lord Molesworth of St Custard's or anywhere you like. Are we, you know, on the same page on this one?

NIGEL   Can you still do that, wangle honours like in the old days?

CHARLES Of course I can do that. Not directly you

understand, but there are still ways and means. One still has access, if you follow my drift.

GEORGE   Take it. Take the title and run, that's my motto. We can always cash in on that one later.

CHARLES   Who's that?

NIGEL   My brother George. The one who almost didn't let you in. You could give the gong and all the baubles to George here, I'm sure he wouldn't say no. And it would finally pay off a debt I owe him.

GEORGE   I'll go with that. Sir George Molesworth, yes, sir. Three bags full, sir. Might even find a wife now. Lady M. And not Lady Muck.

CHARLES   Well, alright, if you're serious and that's what it takes to avoid the referenda. But he's hardly a shining example of the knighthood. Mind you, take a look at some of the others. Look, I must go now, these blasted World Wide Fund people keep hassling me to take over from my father. I just don't have time, and anyway can't be doing this sort of thing these days. Above the fray is where I have to stay, or so they keep advising me. We've got head-hunters searching far and wide for this job, but finding just the right person looks like mission impossible.

GEORGE   Well, don't look at me.

CHARLES   I wasn't going to. But Nigel, if you come across anybody suitable steer them my way. And remember our arrangement, Sir George Molesworth in exchange for a government. Any government as long as there are no referenda. The stakes could not be higher. Some might say the future of our civilisation depends upon it. Are we generally drifting along together on this one?

NIGEL   Generally, most probably. Drifting, almost certainly. I'll do my best.

CHARLES   Will it be good enough?

NIGEL   There's always a first time.

CHARLES   You speak in riddles, but this is serious. I must have certainties.

NIGEL   Then I will certainly do my best.

(Charles leaves)

NIGEL   George, time to round them all up. First get the three Nats to meet me down at the Hole-in-One, and then let's have a St. Custard's party round here. In the meantime, let's try and find the M25 guy.

ACT TWO

Scene 1

In a secret exterior location SHEILA, ROWENA and MARJORY are waiting for NIGEL.

ROWENA Is he always late?

MARJORY I don't know, I've never met him before.

ROWENA And why are we meeting him here of all places?

MARJORY He said it's a top secret spot where no-one ever comes. It's called the Hole-in-One, I don't know why before you ask. Well, I'm expecting some good news, aren't we all?

SHEILA About independence?

MARJORY Yes, Sheila, about independence, what else? He's done the sums, same as we have. He wants our MPs, we want referendums. It's a simple enough bargain to strike, even for him.

SHEILA Devil's bargain for the English.

ROWENA That's their problem. But who goes first, that's what I want to know?

MARJORY   Goes first with what?

ROWENA   With a referendum, natch. I think Sheila is most likely to win in Ulster. If she does, that will set the scene for the rest of us to follow.

SHEILA   I'm sure to win, I just have to run. I've got the wind behind me now, that's sure enough.

MARJORY   Oh no you don't, I think we'll go first. Good God, the Scots have been at it the longest. It's only fair we go first. I'm amazed we're even discussing it.

SHEILA   But you're bound to lose and mess it up for the rest of us. I'm the favourite among us to win. The Scots may hate the English, but they love their pockets even more. Everyone knows that, the whole world over.

ROWENA   She's right, Marjory, the Scots depend on the English for everything, and they know it, even if they'll never admit it. You're sure to lose and you'll mess it up for Sheila, and for me.

MARJORY   You two can keep your bickering to yourselves, we invented independence. America, India, Africa, all because of the Scots and you can't take that away from us, whatever happens. And you know something? It doesn't really matter if we lose, it keeps the party together, we need the cause, that's what we are. A local government with a national cause. We're a cause first, a party second and if it ever happens, a national government third.

ROWENA   You could say we are the same, only more so. But I wouldn't say that. But think about this. If we go first, and we are certain to lose, and heavily too, at least it will establish a precedent that you can both use. One of you might be third time, lucky, i.e. Sheila.

SHEILA   We're never going to agree, let's settle it through Rock, Paper, Scissors. It's as good a way as any.

MARJORY   Isn't that a bit childish? But alright, I'll agree as long as we win.

(The three form a circle).

If you want to play Rock, Paper, Scissors with a group of 2 or more people it is very simple, everyone in the group plays a gesture and if all 3 gestures are showing everyone plays again. If only 2 gestures are showing the players showing the greater gesture stay the other leave the circle.

(Just as they are starting, Nigel appears)

NIGEL   Sorry I'm late. What are you doing?

MARJORY   We are playing Rock, Paper, Scissors to decide which indy ref happens first. But we all know it has to be ours. That's why you're here, isn't it? To do a deal, to do *the* deal, the deal to set us all free from the yoke of English hegemony.

NIGEL   No.

SHEILA   No?

NIGEL   No.

ROWENA   So no deal?

NIGEL   No deal.

MARJORY   So why all the secrecy about this meeting, this Hole-in-One?

NIGEL   Because I'm going to offer you something more, a seat in the all-UK government. Top table.

MARJORY   But we don't want a seat in British government, do we girls? We want independence from the British government. That's the whole point. Haven't you been listening? You're worse than a man.

NIGEL   No, Independence from the British government is not what you want. You might dress it up like that for the voters, and I more than most people understand exactly what you're doing, and why. What you really want is power and money. You can spin it out however you like, but it all comes back to power and money. I can give you both. Let's say by some miracle you win your referendums, then what? Your parties are over, they only exist to push for independence, once you've won, you've lost. You've lost your power. And then there's the other thing.

MARJORY   Money. Lovely money.

NIGEL   Exactamundo. Lovely money. All parties need money, there's never enough. If not for the party, then for those that run them.

ROWENA   We certainly do, we're broke.

NIGEL   Of course you are, you've got no box office. At least Sheila has got some box office, even if it's a fairy story told from afar. Marjory has the box office, but an insatiable appetite to go with it. But, if you green up your messages I can guarantee you each a million pounds a year.

ROWENA   Where from?

NIGEL   It's clean, it's Davos money.

MARJORY   OK. No problem with more money, clean or not. Forget I said that. But that's dependent on us being at your so-called top table, right?

NIGEL   Right.

MARJORY   But with just the four of us, we haven't got the numbers.

NIGEL   We have if we include the Greens, the Cornish loonies, the mad Yorkies and the M25 guy. More than enough.

MARJORY   OK. So you will be Prime Minister, obviously, and the rest of us, what will we be?

NIGEL   Wrong again, Marjory. Rowena will be Prime Minister. You will be Foreign and Commonwealth Secretary and Sheila will be Home Secretary.

ROWENA   But Prime Minister, why me of all people?

NIGEL   Because you are the only one the English will accept. Let's face it, the Welsh are just watered down English, so no problem there.

SHEILA   And me Home Secretary, heavens above why me? Of all people.

NIGEL   Because the English have a keen sense of irony, and home rule from Dublin, even if

we are not quite there yet, rings all the right
bells.

MARJORY I don't mind being Foreign Secretary if it
means a million pounds in the bank. That's a
million every year, right? And we decide who
it's paid to.

NIGEL Right.

ROWENA But you've missed one out. Two out actually,
with the Greens. They did well. I mean
Chancellor of the Exchequer, that's a big one
from what I've heard.

NIGEL That will be the M25 guy, I've already squared
him off. He actually worked in the bank once,
as a clerk I think. And the Greens, that's easy
enough, Basile Fotherington-Thomas will
be in charge of saving us from ourselves,
Minister of the Environment.

SHEILA And you Nigel, what about you?

MARJORY Yes, I was about to ask, what's your game in
all of this?

ROWENA Yeah, come to think of it, what's in it for you?

NIGEL I'll not play any part in government, but I will
be the official historian, with Access All Areas,
and full copyright and intellectual property

rights control. If I'm correct, we are about to live through a very interesting period of history.

ROWENA And as Prime Minister does my cabinet have any policies, or is that too much to ask?

NIGEL No referendums in the first parliament is the only one. That's a deal I've done that you don't need to know about, but one I intend to stick to. And I do stick to my deals once they're agreed.

MARJORY But policies, if Rowena is in charge, she must have some policies, doesn't she?

NIGEL Ideally I'd like you to carry out the Cynical Tendency's Abstract Aims, but none of you have the nous to do that properly. But at least take a look at them.

ROWENA Seems to me like we don't have any other options.

NIGEL You're right, you don't. Not if you want the money, not if you want Power. One other thing, this is all top secret for now, I still haven't squared off the Cornish loonies and the mad Yorkies. Agreed?

ROWENA OK with me.

SHEILA   Me too, mum's the word.

MARJORY   Lips are sealed. This could all work out quite
               well. Quite well indeed.

NIGEL   Agreed, but it's important, no leaks until I've
               sewn up all the loose ends. Understood?

SHEILA   Not a squeak.

MARJORY   Not even a whisper.

ROWENA   Not even from me.

Scene 2

*In the same set/secret exterior location GRABBER and
PEASON are waiting for CHARLES..*

(Grabber enters first from left, then Peason from right.)

GRABBER   Fuck me, what are you doing here?

PEASON   I might ask you the same question. Without
               the bad language, thank you very much.

GRABBER   I'm waiting for my King.

PEASON   Same here. He's my King too, Grabber. He
               said this was a top secret spot where no-one
               ever comes.

(Awkward pause)

PEASON   Is he always late? Not that I'm being impatient.

GRABBER   I see him every week at Buckingham Palace and I'm on time, so he's on time. I'm more important than he is, but I have to go through the motions. What we are doing here, what you are doing here, I have no idea? Actually, I do, and the answer is 'no'.

(Charles arrives)

CHARLES   Gentlemen, sorry I'm late, had trouble finding it. It's so secret I forgot where it is.

GRABBER   Sir, with all due respect, can you explain why Peason is here? I hope it's not what I think it is. Can't we come to some arrangement between us, without any insignificant third parties like Peason being involved?

CHARLES   Gentlemen please. This is the time to stop your traditional squabbling. There are skins to be saved, yours and mine and the country's of course. Always the country first.

PEASON   Always, sir, that goes without saying.

GRABBER   Well, up to a point. One needs to be open-minded about these things. What's brought all this on, sir?

CHARLES I bring disturbing news. Your old school friend Nigel Molesworth has cooked up a scheme whereby Rowena Jones is to be Prime Minister, Sheila O'Flattery is the new Home Secretary, Marjory McDougal of all ghastly people is made Foreign Secretary, Basile Fotherington-Thomas is our Minister of the Environment and the M25 chappie is Chancellor of the Exchequer. He's talking to the Cornish loonies, the mad Yorkies and the LibDems Stalinists as we speak. Quite the straight flush. His agenda is his Abstract Aims, that at least is good news.

GRABBER What are these ridiculous Abstract Aims? He's even threatened me with them.

CHARLES Mostly things I go along with, privately of course these days: Universal Basic Income, positive money, flat taxes, abolish DEFRA, but then he wants to abandon net zero, says it's unaffordable. Whatever that means. And irrelevant, something about the rest of the world. I don't think he shares our vision of doom, unfortunately.

PEASON Sorry sir, but how do you know they are planning all this?

CHARLES Rowena Jones put it all on her Twitter after their meeting. The one where they cooked all this up, well, Nigel cooked it all up. I suspect the others wouldn't have the nous. MI7 told me about it and I told them to take it down. Which they did, gives us a bit of time to come up with something better.

GRABBER I'll crush that weasel Molesworth when I get my hands on him.

CHARLES What's really annoying is that Molesworth promised me there'll be no referenda, and now look what he's done.

PEASON But he's kept his promise, sir. Can't you see what he's done? He's leapfrogged his promise; there will be no referenda. Good old Nigel. He's put them all into power to neutralise them instead. He's actually done you a favour, if keeping the union together is what this is all about.

CHARLES Of course this is what this is all about. That's why I've brought you two together. If it's true politics is about the numbers, you can do the maths of your votes better than I can. You two must get together, put aside your differences and save us all.

GRABBER The bastard!

PEASON Who's that?

GRABBER Who's that, you moron. Molesworth. He's monetising the cock-up. I know his game,

I'd be doing the same in his shoes. The crafty bastard. He's put together the worst management team he can imagine, guaranteed to screw everything up, and I bet you he's lining up a book deal, or more likely an Amazon Prime video deal right now. Right now. The lousy skunk, he won't get away with this, not if I've got anything to do with it. What is he minister of?

CHARLES   According to Jones's tweet, he's not minister of anything, he's the official historian or archivist.

GRABBER   Of course he is. That will be it, I bet he's tied up the copyright and all the intellectual property as well. Government as a reality TV show. I'll soon find out, I own his management company. Which means at least I get a cut. But I'd make more money still being Prime Minister. It's a hard one. I might actually be better off earning commish off Molesworth. I could probably do a better deal for him that he could do for himself.

CHARLES   Exactly why I bought you two together. You need to work together for the sake of the kingdom and the union – the United Kingdom – form a coalition government. You can split the ministries up between you, that's up to you, but you must promise me no referenda during this parliament. And at least take a look at the Abstract Aims, they are not all bad.

PEASON   I don't think I can, sir.

GRABBER   What can't you do now? Sir.

PEASON   You see, it's exactly that type of attitude. 'What can't you do now?' How can we work together, when we can't even have a civil conversation?

GRABBER   It's easy. We are politicians. You loathe me for being a greedy money-making machine and I despise you for being an insincere loser, so we're on an equal footing right from the start. One thing is for sure, I'm going to be Prime Minister, you can be whatever you like. Something out of harm's way would be best, Minister of No Hopers. If there isn't one I'll invent one for you. Then we'll split up the ministries tick tack toe.

PEASON   That's not fair. If it's a coalition, why should you be Prime Minister? Why can't it be me? And you can be whatever you like? You don't understand, I've waited all my life to be Prime Minister.

GRABBER   Because, 1) my party's got more votes than your party. Because 2) I'm already Prime Minister and you've never had a job in your life. And because 3) I'm good at it and you'd be completely useless. Shall I go on?

PEASON   But you can't govern without my support. The numbers again.

GRABBER   That's true. I've given you plenty of stick, and now I'm going to give you a carrot. I know all about your party's finances. This election has just about cleaned you out, and you couldn't fight another one for at least two years, maybe three. You're basically dependent on the public sector unions for your income, and half their members are up in arms about it. They love me more than they love you, unsurprisingly. Am I right?

PEASON   You might be, I haven't really checked.

GRABBER   Of course you haven't checked, you're Peason, and of course I have, I'm Grabber. Now you listen to me. Here's the deal. Your party is sponsoring the bill which, with the backing of all these other new cartoon parties, will certainly go through parliament.

PEASON   The Foreign Donations Transparency Bill, it's the jewel in our crown, very much my own doing. I'm proud of it, very proud.

GRABBER   Why doesn't that surprise me? It's a prig's charter. If you pull out of that Bill, it will die. So you do pull out, join me in a coalition, with me as Prime Minister. You can be whatever else you like, Defence if you want to make a few bob, Foreign if you want to fuck off around the world, and I'll double your party's income every year for as long as our coalition lasts.

PEASON   You mean double it with these anonymous overseas donations I'm trying to ban?

GRABBER   Oh, you are quick today. Of course, only you and I will know the secret of the little arrangement, you and His Majesty here of course. If I may speak for His Majesty, he is the very soul of discretion. Are you not, sir?

CHARLES   I am. And I believe it's called an offer you can't refuse, Mr Peason.

GRABBER   That's one way of putting it, sir. I prefer to call it business as usual. But as always there is a snag.

PEASON   My integrity?

GRABBER   Don't make me laugh. Your integrity ranks alongside your sincerity, Tory boy. i.e. not very highly! No, what I mean is your great friend Nigel Molesworth and his gang of misfits are going to be shafted. Big time. Where it hurts. That's your choice, lasting friendship or money and power.

CHARLES   Enough Mr. Grabber. Mr. Peason is too nice to say so, so I'll say it for him. Money and power. And the union, of course, that's the main thing.

Scene 3

In the same set/secret exterior location NIGEL and BASILE meet.

(Nigel enters first from left, then Basile from right. They kiss both cheeks)

NIGEL   Houston, we have a problem.

BASILE   Oh dear.

NIGEL   By the way, why are we meeting here?

BASILE   It's my top secret spot where no-one ever comes.

NIGEL   OK, back to the problem. Yes, oh dear. Our little plan to have the nutters run the government and you save the planet has come off the rails.

BASILE   It's crashed?

NIGEL   It's crashed. Rowena tweeted it when I asked her not to, that was picked up immediately by MI7, they told the King, the King told them to take it down, which they did, and the

King has now cobbled together a deal with Grabber and Peason. We are out in the cold.

BASILE How do you know this?

NIGEL I've got high placed moles in both the Grabber and Peason camps, they both said the same, so I'm inclined to believe it.

BASILE But Grabber and Peason hate each other. I don't like to use the word *hate* Nigel, but they do. Hate each other. Horrible just to think about it. Oh, Nigel, what shall we do?

NIGEL Hate each other they do, but they love money and power even more. But there might be a Plan B, or actually Plan E.

BASILE Ooh, I knew you'd think of something, Nigel. I can't think of anything when I get in a fluster. Sometimes, I just have to lie down and wait for the moment to pass. Do you ever get one of those turns? No, I don't suppose you do, they affect me terribly.

NIGEL No, can't say I do. Nothing wrong with them, they just passed me by. Plan E, I'm still at the thinking aloud stage. You know your Davos funders, what are they called?

BASILE The Global Settlement Foundation. From Oslo of all places. They are very upright, too upright for many people no doubt, but I can vouch for them. Most certainly they've never missed a payment, always asking if I want more. Of course I don't, but still, it's nice of them to ask, they're so considerate.

NIGEL   I'm sure all you say is true, my friend. Tell me more about what they want.

BASILE   You remember the Covid pandemic?

NIGEL   Only too well. Everyone obeyed the government even when there was no scientific evidence that it was as bad as they said. Just fantasy computer modelling by vested interests. The government believed it, the media believed the government, and the people believed the media. Fear, loathing and panic – game, set and match to the bad guys.

BASILE   Well, *I* believed it. At the time. Why wouldn't I?

NIGEL   Because you believe what you're told without asking why you've been told it. The media have been bought by government advertising and sold for survival by clickbait. They're not interested in the truth, and asking awkward questions to find out the truth. All doubters like me were rubbished by the same media that should've been asking the same questions I was asking, instead of asking questions to feed their own egos.

BASILE   Well, be that as it may, the good guys want to do the same again, but not have everyone stay indoors like before. This time it's even better, to control how everyone spends their money so that they can save the planet that way.

NIGEL   As I've been saying all along.

BASILE   Oh Nigel, it's so clever, the technology is absolutely amazing. There's this social credit system. I saw it all in Oslo on this wonderful presentation they gave us. So, let's say you spend your money filling up your Rolls-Royce, naughty Nigel, you get minus credits, but if you spend it recharging your Tesla, nice Nigel, you get plus credits. It's called social credit and they say it's for the best, for all our futures.

NIGEL   I know the score. Next up, if there's something in short supply, the person with the better social credit gets the tickets. It's clever tech all right, that's the only good thing about. They can keep anything they want that you want in short supply. A few knock-backs then slowly but surely you learn to comply. That's where we are heading. Pavlov comes to mind.

BASILE   The chap with the dogs! Yes, that's right. They do it in China, it works wonderfully, and China has really cut down on pollution as a result. They showed me these graphs. And they do it all just to stop us all becoming extinct, that's the only other option. It's so kind and thoughtful of them, thank heavens somebody cares so much.

NIGEL   Have you met the head man or woman yet?

BASILE   Yes, he's really nice. You'd love him. Quite visionary. Karl Schmidt, he is also chairman of the World Economic Forum, that's the Davos connection. You can ski there in winter, and hike in summer. They even have a music festival. But Karl, he hasn't long to go.

NIGEL   He's retiring, isn't he? Quite soon I read. No known successor yet?

BASILE   No, not that I've heard of. I mean they are all billionaires. Someone has even called it the billionaires club. Even I'm not in that league. But Americans count billions differently from us, did you know that Nigel?

NIGEL   I've heard it on the gripevine. Grabber will know him for sure.

BASILE   Nigel, I can hear your clever clogs turning topsides. You mean Grabber could take over from him?

NIGEL   It's a thought, isn't it? Grabber would be ideal. He's already a billionaire, so he's in the club. His natural instinct is to monetise anything that moves, so that's a season ticket. He likes control and power as much as money, and then he can have all three.

BASILE   But we've always said he's a revolting human being. Which he is. I'm not sure he'd fit in, Nigel. These people are all so nice, they're really nice.

NIGEL   Oh, he can be nice enough when it suits him, I've seen it. If you can put in a good word for Grabber, put him on their radar, I can probably get rid of Peason. Then we are back to Plan E, via Plan F.

BASILE   I'll try of course. They listen to me that's for sure. Unlike certain other parties I could mention, Mr Peason. How can you get rid of him as you put it?

NIGEL   Peason? Through my YouTube connections. YouTube and I both make a fortune out of each other. Google own YouTube, so ...

BASILE   They do? I never knew that. Everyone owns everything these days.

NIGEL   I'll tell Google they need a political insider as a global advisor, someone who will tow the party line and smile sincerely whenever needed. Peason would be ideal. I can at least plant the seed right at the top of Google, probably do a bit more than that, chuck some fertiliser on it too.

BASILE   Oh Nigel, you're so clever. Always scheming. How do you do it?

NIGEL   Unfortunately, it comes naturally. But you know, I am getting a bit fed up with all of this.

BASILE   How come? You seem to have it all.

NIGEL   I look at you and think, why aren't I a bit more like my old friend Basile. Not a care in the world, happy in his own skin, sorry *her* own skin, always optimistic, never cynical, trusting. Naïve, if you don't mind me saying so, but what's wrong with that?

BASILE   But Nigel, you can't change now. Everyone knows Nigel. Some people love Nigel, some people don't. I love Nigel. You're Nigel, a national treasure just as you are.

NIGEL   Yes, well a national treasure who just can't help himself. But keep that to yourself.

⟞⟝

Scene 4

At Nigel's flat, GEORGE alone, sitting, picking his nose. Soon MARJORY enters.

(Door phone rings)

GEORGE Arise, Sir George.

(Answers)

> Come on up.

(Marjory enters)

> You alone?

MARJORY Yes, the others sent me here on my own. Is Nigel in?

GEORGE Nigel is organising a St. Custard's school reunion. Top secret. So I haven't just told you.

MARJORY Never heard a word you said. When is he back?

GEORGE Not for the rest of the day, I think he's going to see the King after that.

MARJORY Heavens, what's he up to now? I'm on the 18.30 flight back home, can you pass on what I'm about to tell you?

GEORGE Sure, fire away.

MARJORY   Do you need to write it down?

GEORGE   Do I look like a blinking thickie?

MARJORY   Yes, and you act like one too. Never mind, you'll have to do and try not to mess it up, laddie. Sheila, Rowena and I have been thinking about what Nigel proposed, you know that we green up our agendas in exchange for secure funding and then we take over the great offices of state.

GEORGE   Sounds good to me. Is there a problem?

MARJORY   Yes. We can't do it.

GEORGE   Which bit can't you do? Take the money or run the government?

MARJORY   Run the government, obviously.

GEORGE   Well, it can't be that difficult. As Nigel would say, look at the clowns who are doing it now.

MARJORY   Well, it's easy to say that, but he wants Rowena to be PM, and Rowena has never actually had a job as such, let alone run anything, except of course for Plaid Cymru. And they're a shower of shite, pardon my French. She left school at 16, joined the trade union, became a shop steward, then ran the union branch, then the whole union, then

Plaid Cymru and now she's an MP. She's got more front than Hastings, but even she's getting nervous about being Prime Minister.

GEORGE   Oh, then what about Sheila?

MARJORY   Same thing really. She's never had a job either. She's been a poet and a folk singer, a good one too. She's waited in the family restaurant in Fermanagh when she's been desperate. She is a dreamer, but one with the gift of the gab. A big time gift of the gab. But as she told me this morning, the only decision she's ever made is which particular rabble to rouse.

GEORGE   And you're the same I suppose, only good for rabble rousing?

MARJORY   If this conversation wasn't so serious, I would take that as the insult I'm sure you meant it to be. Of course I'm not like the others, I've had far more experience of politics and life. OK, I've never had what you might call a job, but I have been running my political party and local government for 10 years. That I can assure you, is no easy option, dealing with the infighting and backstabbing. It's not for the faint hearted. And I'm not faint hearted, I'm brave hearted like a good Scot, but I can't be brave hearted and fighting for independence if I'm part of the establishment I'm trying to be independent from. The whole movement would collapse. Our existing funders would vanish. And I can't upset our existing funds for reasons you don't need to know about. Nor Nigel. And that's what we are, a movement. We're not a national government, and if we tried to be one it would be the end of us. I can see all that, even if the others can't.

GEORGE   But what about the new money?

MARJORY   That's what I want to talk to Nigel about as well. If there's a way we can keep the new money if we drop out of the government side of things.

GEORGE   I don't know, you'll have to speak to him about that. But I thought that was the deal, wasn't it?

MARJORY   It was. Do you know where he's getting the money from?

GEORGE   Not exactly, I overheard it had something to do with Davos, whatever that is.

MARJORY   Yes, he said. That will be the World Economic Forum. It's a billionaires club. That's what seeming to be going green in a manifesto was all about.

GEORGE   What's that got to do with going green?

MARJORY It's window dressing for CBDC.

GEORGE Sounds like a night club.

MARJORY Good God, George, which planet do you live on? Central bank digital currency. No more cash. They'll know exactly what you're doing every moment of every day, and they can monetise that by predicting what you're about to do next.

GEORGE Sounds fair enough to me. So why do you want to take the money, if it's such a bad thing?

MARJORY Oh George, George. Actually, that's a very good question, for which I don't have an answer. Let's just call it politics. Power. I need to stay in power, and to stay in power I need money. Does that answer your question?

GEORGE I suppose so. Anyway, back to Nigel, the message is you want to pull out of the deal but you want to keep the dosh, right?

MARJORY Well, you might find a more elegant way of framing that, George. How about: while we appreciate his kind offer of important and crucial roles in government, we need more time to prepare ourselves for these significant undertakings for the public good and in the interim we could use his equally kind offer of funding to facilitate our continuous development as we take on the additional and essential *ad hoc* and *de facto* practical training and experience that are needed to help us prepare for these important roles in the fullness of time.

GEORGE   I can't understand a word of that gobbledygook. You want to have your cake and eat it, right?

MARJORY   Just do your best, George. I've got to catch the flight. Ask Nigel to call me tomorrow.

Scene 5
At Nigel's flat, GRABBER and BASILE in one conversation, NIGEL and PEASON in another.

(GEORGE enters tinging a glass for attention)

GEORGE   Quiet everybody, my brother Nigel has something to say.

NIGEL   Friends and… well, just friends. These last few, strange days since the election have brought us all together, and shown that whatever else we are, after all still old St. Custardians. So it is my old school chums that I want to be the first to hear my news, news of my change of heart, change of direction. But before telling you my news, maybe some of you have your own news, which I'm sure will be far more interesting than mine.

GRABBER   You can say that again. Whatever news you have Molesworth 1, mine is far more important. For many years now I have been attending the World Economic Forum in Davos, where even if I say so myself, the world's other billionaires and political impresarios have listened with great attention to my well-considered views on monetary systems and more recently the need for environmental control, and how we can clean up in both senses. It was hardly surprising to me, therefore, that the outgoing Chairman, Karl Schmidt, rang me the other day and personally insisted that I take over from him when he retires. The opportunities for self-enrichment should be obvious to all, and they certainly were to his board of trustees who have my full support in the support for me. Therefore, as of next week, I shall no longer be either Prime Minister or leader of the Conservative Party. But I have many other skills, too many to mention, and I have used another one of them to help another old St. Custardian here tonight. No, not you Molesworth 1, I'm talking about Molesworth 2. I asked Molesworth 1 if he knew any good thugs and he's found me one. Tell them, lad.

GEORGE　It's true, and I was going to tell you later Bro, but the news has only just come through. Grabber here has made me headmaster of the new St. Custard's. He said he needed to find a good thug to run it, and now he has found one. Me. It's still a penal colony like Nigel always said it was, but it's now an official government one and Grabber owns it and he's put me in charge. I'm now the head beak. So all the squirts and weeds better watch out.

PEASON　Well, well done George. It looks like all change all round. I too had a phone call, most unexpectedly. From Sophie Macpherson Ltd, the international headhunters, the Los Angeles branch. You'll never guess what they want me to be? Me of all people?

NIGEL　Tim, we're never going to guess, so why don't you just tell us?

PEASON　It's going to mean giving up being leader of the Labour Party.

GRABBER　Who cares? What is it?

PEASON　And I'm going to have to live in Palo Alto, that's a swish tech suburb of San Francisco, apparently.

NIGEL　Tim!

PEASON Very well, it's nothing less than Google itself. I'm to be Vice-President of Global Affairs and Communications. I had no idea they were even looking and even if I had I wouldn't have thought of applying. And the salary! Think big figures I never dreamed of. Perks too, I get my own assistant. And my own office. So I'm thrilled, and Sarah is too. But there's one condition.

GRABBER I knew it, a snag. What is it?

PEASON They want me to be a knight, Sir Timothy Peason. They say it looks better for the optics, and a lot of my job is about optics. I'm not quite sure what they mean by optics, but I think it means how everything looks. That matters to them as much as I do, apparently. The two must go together.

NIGEL I can arrange that with the King.

PEASON Excellent, then I am Sir Timothy Peason of Silicon Valley, and as far as I'm concerned the Labour Party can do the other thing.

BASILE Congratulations Peason, and to you too Grabber. And to you, dear George. You were always such a wonderful thug. But I've got big news too, even bigger news than either of you three.

(Pause for effect)

NIGEL　　Well, Basile, out with it now!

BASILE　　King Charles himself has put me in charge of the World Wildlife Fund. To replace his father, the sainted Prince Philip. Well, I don't know if the King did that personally, but he certainly must have put in a good word for me. And someone must have put in a good word to the King, otherwise how would he know I was interested in the job? Which I wasn't in all fairness. Never even knew there was a vacancy. But now I've got it, I'm so happy. Of course I'll have to give up the Green Party, but honestly recently there's been so much infighting about the so-called New Reality, I don't know where we stand if the world isn't going to end. That was always what appealed to me most about the Green party, the end of the world. And anyway I've always loved pandas. You remember when we all started at St. Custard's, first thing was matron confiscated all our cuddly toys, you all had 50 teddy bears, I had a panda. I think it was a boy, but I called it Maureen anyway.

NIGEL　　Congratulations to you too, Basile, I think you'll be marvellous. What would old Grimes say now of us old St. Custardians? One in charge of the World Economic Forum, really in charge of all our futures, one in charge of a Big Tech giant's face to the world, one in charge of preserving the world's endangered species, one in charge of St. Custard's itself and one the UK Prime Minister.

GRABBER   No, Molesworth 1, I said I would have to quit being Prime Minister if I'm ruling the world.

PEASON   Me too, Nigel, I'd be the natural one to take over from Grabber, but I'm out of UK politics too.

BASILE   Oh dear, I do hope you don't think it's me, Nigel. If I'm in charge of pandas I can't run the country too.

GEORGE   Well, you can count me out.

(Pause)

ALL FOUR AS ONE   You?!

NIGEL   Yes, me. It's been coming to me slowly over the last few days. I've made a career from being a cynic, but now I see you real politicos up close I see I was all mouth and no trousers, whereas you lot are nothing but trousers. And the three Nats are just as bad, as is the King, the mad Yorkies, the Cornish loonies and even the M25 guy. I don't know, but I think against all the odds something good might come out of this with you three all gone.

PEASON   Nigel, that's not very nice.

GRABBER   It's a damn slander is what it is.

BASILE   I hope you don't include me.

GEORGE   Or me.

NIGEL   Fellow St. Custardians, for once, let's give hope a try. If you will all row in your MPs behind me, and choose whoever you want as cabinet minister tick, tack, toe, plus we find room for the mad Yorkies, the Cornish loonies and the M25 guy, even find room for the LibDem Stalinists, we can have a government of national unity. Everyone pulling in the same direction. The King behind it too.

GRABBER   It's your Abstract Aims again isn't it, Molesworth? All of a sudden the great cynic is a naive idealist. It will never work.

PEASON   I worry for you Nigel, you're just not cut out for any form of responsibility like I am.

BASILE   He's right Nigel. It's a viper's nest is Westminster, go back to YouTube. You were such a hit, they all loved you. Now they'll all hate you, just like they hate us.

GEORGE   They are all right, Bro, don't bother, just take the money and run like before.

NIGEL   I thank you all for your advise, and you may well be right. But why not give it a chance? Nothing else has worked. Now that I'm the only game in town, now that I've moved you all on to... sorry, now that you've all moved on to the bigger and better things, so now that I'm the only possible option for Prime Minister, what do you all say? Can you at least call me Prime Minister.

GRABBER   If I must. Prime Minister, there I've said it.

PEASON   Alright, Nigel, Prime Minister.

BASILE   Prime Minister, sounds odd though.

GEORGE   What the hell, Prime Minister.

NIGEL   That wasn't too painful, was it? Now, am I going to fall flat on my face?

ALL FOUR AS ONE   Yes, Prime Minister!